3-D PAPER CRAFTS

by Ron Broda

With Joanne Webb

Photography by Wally Randall

Scholastic Canada Ltd.

Scholastic Canada Ltd.

123 Newkirk Road, Richmond Hill, Ontario, Canada L4C 3G5

Scholastic Inc.

555 Broadway, New York, NY 10022, USA

Scholastic New Zealand Limited

Private Bag 94407, Greenmount, Auckland, New Zealand

Scholastic Australia Pty Limited

PO Box 579, Gosford, NSW 2250, Australia

Scholastic Ltd.

Villiers House, Clarendon Avenue, Leamington Spa, Warwickshire CV32 5PR, UK

Canadian Cataloguing in Publication Data

Broda, Ron
3-D paper crafts

ISBN 0-590-24980-0

1. Paper sculpture – Juvenile literature. 2. Paper
work – Juvenile literature. I. Webb, Joanne. II. Title.
III. Title: Three-D paper crafts.

TT870.B76 1997   j745.54   C96-932164-3

4 3 2 1   Printed in Canada   7 8 9/9

Welcome to the World of Paper Sculpting!

Making pictures and crafts out of paper is an old tradition. It originated in Asia, then spread to Europe and North America. *Sculpting* paper is a relatively new trend, and it's becoming more and more popular.

When I first saw a paper sculpture, I just had to try making one myself. Before I knew it I was hooked. Since then, my hobby has become my job.

Over the years, many kids have asked me, "How do you do that?" This book will let you in on some of my secrets. Start by reading about the tools and techniques I use and give the practice piece a try. Then jump in! For each of these projects, count on a full morning or afternoon of activity.

These paper sculptures look tricky, but they're all fun and easy to make. With a little patience, you'll be rewarded with unusual gifts and decorations. The more you practise, the better you'll get — I guarantee it! Soon you'll be coming up with your own ideas. Let your imagination run wild . . .

All the best,

Ron Broda

Tools

Burnisher: An inexpensive metal tool often used for embossing. You can find one at most craft stores (it might be labelled "embossing tool"), but any tool with a smooth, rounded tip can be used instead. A knitting needle, which is perfect for curling, can also be used as a burnisher. You can try the end of a small paintbrush, as well. Results may vary from tool to tool — experiment until you find the one that works best for you.

Glue: Use all-purpose white glue.

Paper: Be creative with paper! Medium to heavy paper works best, but almost any kind can be used: wrapping paper, writing paper, watercolour paper, handmade paper, Bristol board, etc.

Construction paper is perfect for the beginning paper sculptor because it comes in so many colours, costs very little and is easy to find in craft stores, art supply stores, even

2

drugstores! Its soft texture is ideal for sculpting. All of the projects in this book can be made with construction paper.

Scissors: Safety scissors work fine. If you must use pointy scissors, make sure you have an adult's supervision.

Tracing paper: You can find this at any craft or art supply store.

Sharp pencil: Use this for tracing patterns. It needs to be soft — use a pencil marked HB.

Hole punch: The single-hole kind works best. Use it to punch out small, even circles.

Work pad: Burnishing works best on a soft surface. You can get sheets of craft foam at craft stores, but the reverse side of an old foam-backed placemat or mouse pad will work just as well.

Light: This is a sculptor's best friend. Light brings out all the depth and shadows in a piece — it allows you to really see the results of your work. Take frequent "light breaks" to hold your work by a window or under a lamp. It's a great learning experience.

Techniques

Tracing

▸ First, decide which paper colours you want to work with. Try the colours used in this book or choose your own. Contrasting shades work well together.

▸ Find the pattern pieces for your project in the pattern section in the middle of this book. Take a small piece of tracing paper and place it over one of the patterns. With a sharp pencil, carefully trace solid lines (cutting lines) and all dotted lines (scoring and folding lines). Work on a hard surface so the paper won't rip.

▸ Lay the tracing paper, *pencil side down*, on top of your selected piece of construction paper. Retrace over the markings so that their impression is left clearly on the construction paper. Remove the tracing paper. Now you're ready to cut out the piece.

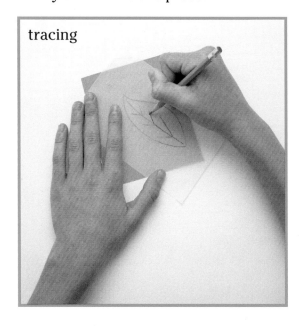

tracing

Cutting

It's a good idea to practise making nice clean cuts before you start. Holding the scissors steady in one hand and the paper in the other, open the scissors wide and start cutting slowly. You'll have the best control if you keep the scissor blades wide apart as you cut. Try cutting a wavy line, then a zig-zag. Hold the scissors in one place and gently change the direction of the *paper* as you cut. Aim for a neat, even cut. When you're comfortable cutting this way, you can move on to project pieces.

cutting

▸ You will find it easiest to keep track of the pieces if you cut and work on only one at a time.

▸ Remember to cut along all solid lines (not the dotted ones).

▸ After cutting, put discarded bits in a separate place so you won't get confused.

- ▸ Your finished piece will have pencil markings on one side (the "pencil side") and be clean on the other (the "clean side"). Throughout this book we will be telling you to place pieces "clean side down" or "clean side up." You'll be flipping the pieces over several times, so it's important to remember which side is which.

- ▸ Once you've cut a piece, be sure to mark its letter *on the pencil side*.

Sculpting Techniques

Burnishing:

This technique makes an indentation on paper. It is especially useful for softening and rounding the edges of paper pieces. To burnish, place a cut piece on the work pad. With medium pressure, slowly outline the edges of the piece. Stay close to the edge, but don't go past it. Aim for a continuous line, rather than a back-and-forth motion. Look at the photo on page 7 for an example of burnishing.

Scoring:

A burnisher is also used to mark a crisp line — a score — on the paper. A score creates a sharp edge for folding and shaping. The project pieces in this book are marked with dotted lines to show you where to score.

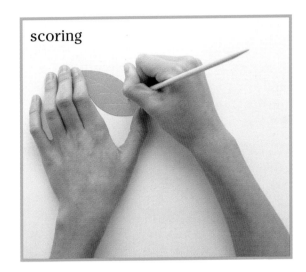

scoring

- ▸ You will sometimes be asked to score on the clean side of a piece. To do this, lightly score *on the pencil side first* to create a guideline, then flip it over and score over the raised line.

- ▸ Don't use your work pad when scoring — a hard surface is best. It will prevent the paper from being torn or dragged.

Curling:

Curling paper is easily done with a knitting needle, pen or pencil. To curl, lay a cut piece on a work pad near the edge of a table. Holding the tool as though it were a dinner knife, rub firmly over the surface of the paper. Sweep the tool back and forth, right to the edges of the piece, until it starts to curl up. See the photo on page 7 for an example of curling.

- ▸ Don't use scissors to curl. They can easily cut the paper — or your fingers.

5

Pinching:

After you've burnished, scored and curled a piece, turn it over, *clean side up*, and look at the result under the light. It is becoming "sculpted" — rounded and three-dimensional! If you feel the piece needs further shaping, gently pinch the edges between your fingers until it looks right.

pinching

Gluing

Take care when gluing — just use tiny dots of glue. If you accidentally put on too much, spread it out thinly with a toothpick (or your finger if it's clean), as though you were spreading butter. Remember, the less glue you use, the neater your finished sculpture will be. The glue will also dry more quickly if you use it sparingly.

▸ To avoid wasting glue, try squeezing about a teaspoon onto a disposable plate and applying it with a toothpick or the tip of a plastic stir-stick. Just add more if it starts to dry out.

▸ For best results, position the piece to be glued *before* you apply any glue. Look at where it's touching the piece it will be attached to — that's where the glue should go.

▸ If you accidentally get glue on your clean side, don't rub at it. Just get most of it off with a toothpick and let it dry.

Common Sense Tips:

▸ Handle tools with care. Make sure you have adult supervision if you're using any sharp tools.

▸ Keep clean: this goes for your hands, your work pad and the surface you're working on. Cover your workspace with an old tablecloth or kraft paper. (Newsprint can smudge your work.)

▸ Don't wreck your parents' dinner table! Score on a firm piece of cardboard to prevent damage.

▸ Give yourself plenty of room to work.

▸ Handle paper gently so it doesn't tear. When sculpting, hold paper down very lightly with just your fingertips.

Follow the steps on the opposite page for a practice run!

Leaf *(A Practice Piece)*

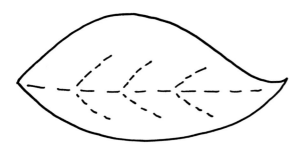

▸ With a pencil, trace the leaf shape on this page. Then place the tracing paper pencil side down over construction paper (use green paper if you want a realistic leaf) and run over the marks firmly with the pencil. Be sure to transfer all pattern markings to the paper.

▸ Carefully **cut** out the leaf shape.

▸ On a hard surface, lightly **score** along all the dotted lines, then turn the piece over, clean side up, and score over the raised lines.

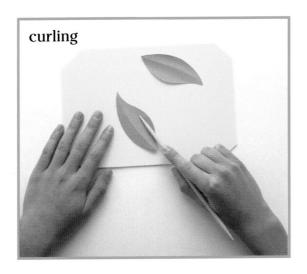
curling

▸ **Pinch** the leaf along the score line.

▸ Now turn the piece clean side down. On a soft work pad, **curl** each half of the leaf separately: holding a knitting needle or similar tool as though it were a dinner knife, rub back and forth over the paper until it starts to curve upward.

▸ Still on the work pad, clean side down, **burnish** around all the edges.

▸ Turn the leaf over, clean side up. Now you're almost there! To complete the leaf, shape it with your fingers until it looks just right to you.

burnishing

Congratulations — you're well on your way to becoming an expert paper sculptor. Now, find a project in this book that interests you and get started. Have fun!

Madame Butterfly

This colourful butterfly looks as if it has just flown in from the garden!

► With clean sides up, score and fold **A**, **B** and **C** (wings) along dotted lines. Glue **C** to **B**.

► Glue **D** pieces (decorations) to **A**. Punch out paper dots with a hole punch and glue to wings. With clean sides down, curl both halves of top and bottom wings (see photo 1).

► With clean sides down, curl **E** (body) and **F** (head). Score body along dotted line.

► Turn the body clean side up. Holding it steady, curl the antennae up. Glue the head to the body.

► Punch out two eyes with the hole punch. Burnish each eye with a circular motion, from outside to centre. Glue eyes in place.

► With clean side down, put a few small drops of glue on the fold line of **A**. Glue **A** to **B**.

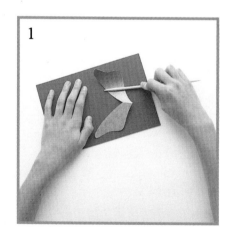

▸ Attach the body to the wings: place a few dots of glue along the edges of **E**, spread it thin, then glue the piece to the wings (see photo 2). Hold in place until dry, about 30 seconds.

Don't worry too much about making "perfect" sculptures. Nature's not perfect, so why should these be?

Gift idea: Find an interesting stone or piece of driftwood and glue your butterfly to it, for an unusual paperweight. Or, decorate a wrapped gift with it, instead of using a bow.

9

Flower Power

*You can decorate a gift with one of these pretty blooms,
or even hide a tiny gift within its petals!*

▸ With clean side down, score **A** (base) along dotted lines. Turn over and rescore lines to add detail and depth. Then curl the 11 base petals, some up and some down.

▸ **B** is the pattern for one petal — trace and cut this shape until you have 34 petals in all! Score them along the dotted lines, then turn them clean side up and score over the raised lines. Set seven petals aside.

▸ Curl the other 27 petals, some up and some down. For a realistic effect, first curl the petal tip, then flip over and curl the petal base (see photo 1).

▸ Now build the flower: Glue all the petals, clean side up, one by one, to **A**. Start at the base, and keeping adding petals side by side until you have a full circle of petals. Then just continue around the circle until all the petals are in place (see photo 2).

▸ Finally, with clean sides up, curl up the last seven petals. Then glue them one by one to the centre of the flower.

▸ If you like, decorate the finished flower with a few copies of **C** (leaf), like the one you made in the practice exercise.

Gift idea: Make a corsage for Mom by gluing on a pin back. Or, glue on a pipe-cleaner "stem" and present the flower to a friend. You can also make a cardboard flower pot like this one. Glue several flowers to a hidden backing and decorate as you wish.

Go Fish!

*There are lots of interesting cutouts
in this sculpture, so remember to cut all the solid lines.*

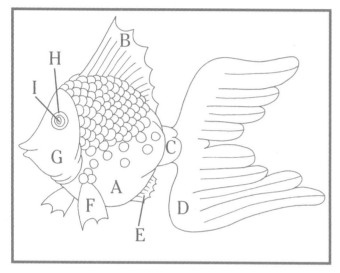

▶ With clean side down, curl **A** (body). Score along dotted line, and burnish around all cut edges.

▶ Now add some fish scales. Punch out paper dots with a hole punch and glue them one by one to **A**, overlapping them (see photo 1).

▶ Spread a few drops of glue across the bottom edges of the cut strips of **B** (dorsal fin). Then slip the fin into the notch on the top of **A** and hold in place until dry.

▶ With clean side down, curl **C** and burnish around all edges. Glue behind **A**.

▶ With clean side down, curl **D** (tail fin). Curl strips in alternating directions, to give them a rippled, swimming-in-water look.

Burnish around all edges. Glue behind **C**.

▶ Glue **E** (fin) behind **A**.

▶ With clean sides down, curl both **F** pieces (fins) and glue them to **A**, one in front and one behind.

▶ With clean side down, burnish around all edges of **G** (head). Score along the dotted lines, and burnish the dot.

▶ Now make the fish eye. With clean side down, burnish **H** (outside edge of eye) with a circular motion, from outside to centre (see photo 2).

▶ With a hole punch, punch out a paper dot. Glue it to **H**. Glue **I** (pupil) on top of the punched-out dot, or simply draw one on.

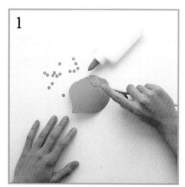

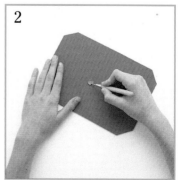

▶ Glue the eye to the raised dot on the head. Glue the head to the body.

Gift idea: Make a mobile! Cover the backs of several fish with paper (so they will look neat when they spin), and glue a paper clip to each one. Tie fishing line, coloured yarn or string to each paper clip, then knot the string around a hoop shape, leaving a long end free. Make the hoop shape out of a coat hanger (ask an adult for help), or use an embroidery hoop or the rim of an aluminum pie plate. Gather the long ends of the strings at the top and knot them together.

Holiday Wreath

This wreath will hold its shape nicely if you use a sturdy paper for the base — try Bristol board.

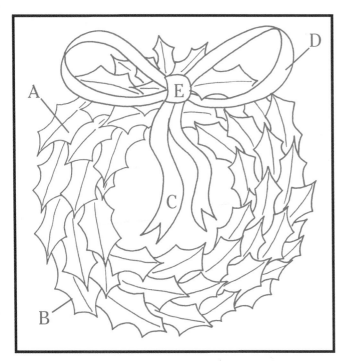

realistic wavy shape. Glue, clean side up, to wreath. Make two loop shapes out of **D** (bow loops) by curling both ends in toward the centre and gluing them in place (see photo 2). Position them as you like on the wreath and glue them in place.

▸ Curl **E** (knot) and glue it into place over the bow loops.

▸ Decorate your wreath with "holly berries": punch out red paper dots with a hole punch and burnish each one with a circular motion, from outside to centre. Glue in place.

▸ Trace and cut about 50 copies of **A** (leaves). With clean side up, score each leaf down the middle. Pinch to shape.

▸ Now build the wreath. Glue the leaves in rows of three to **B** (wreath base). Start each row by gluing one leaf to the outside edge. Then glue one to the inside and one to the middle. Build the rows so that each new row overlaps the last one (see photo 1).

▸ Now add some ribbon. Curl **C** (ribbon), one centimetre-long section at a time — one section clean side up, the next clean side down, and so on, to give the ribbon a

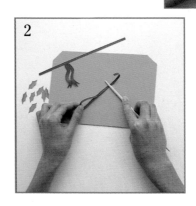

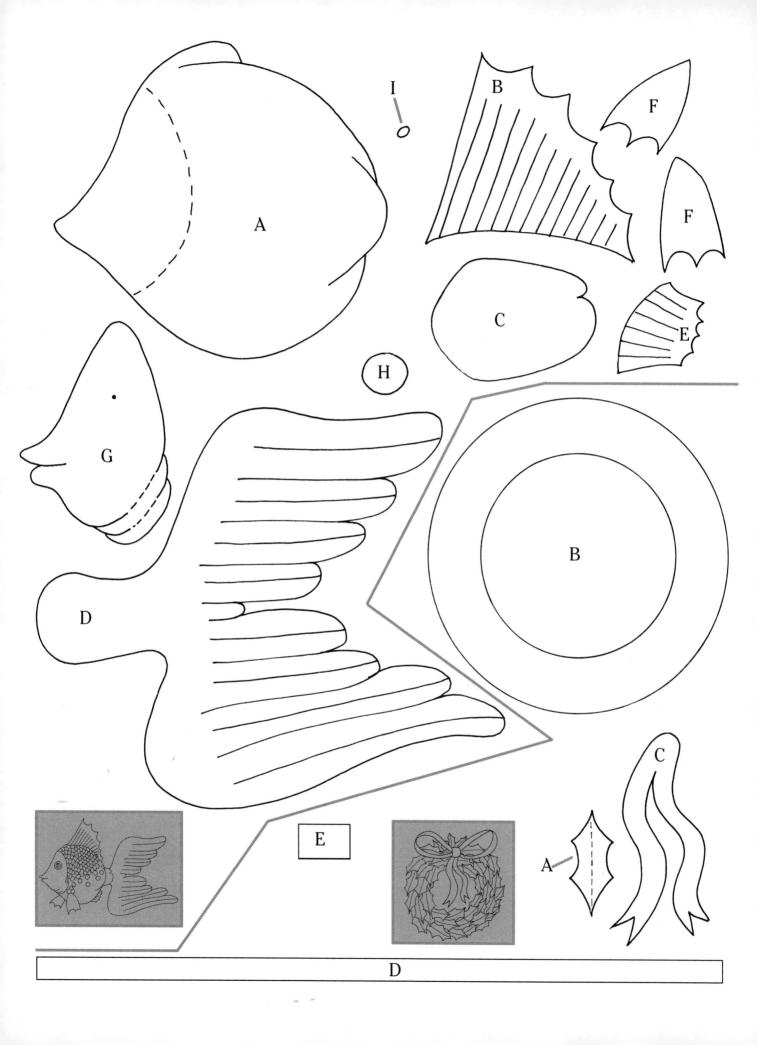

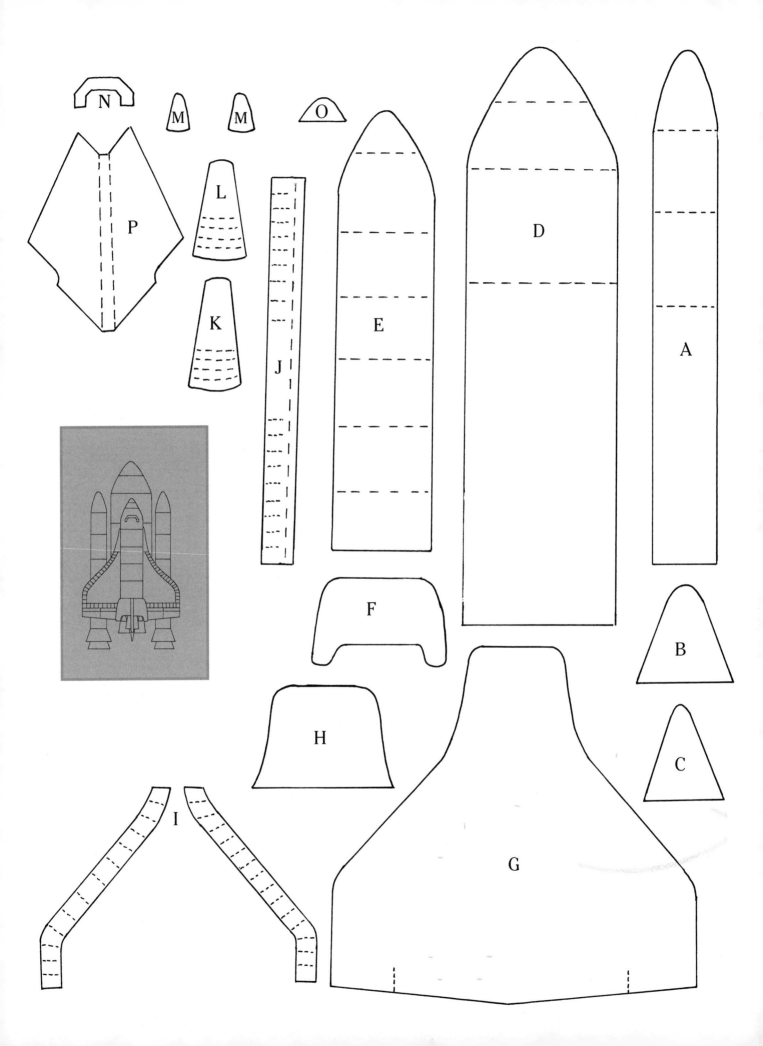

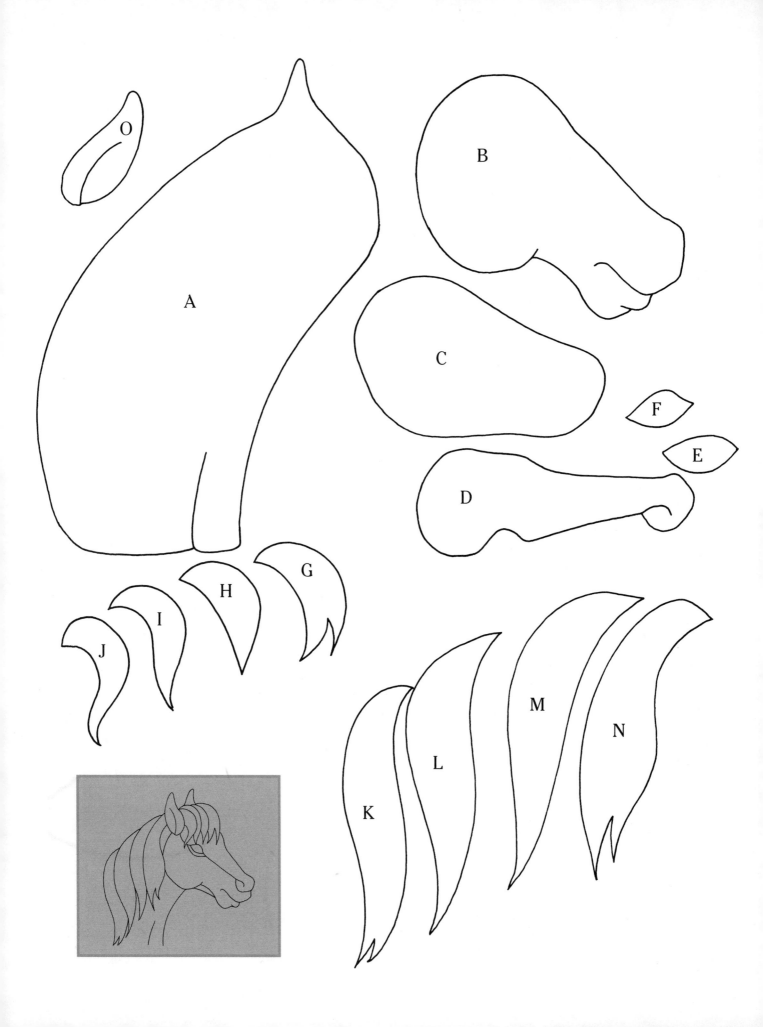

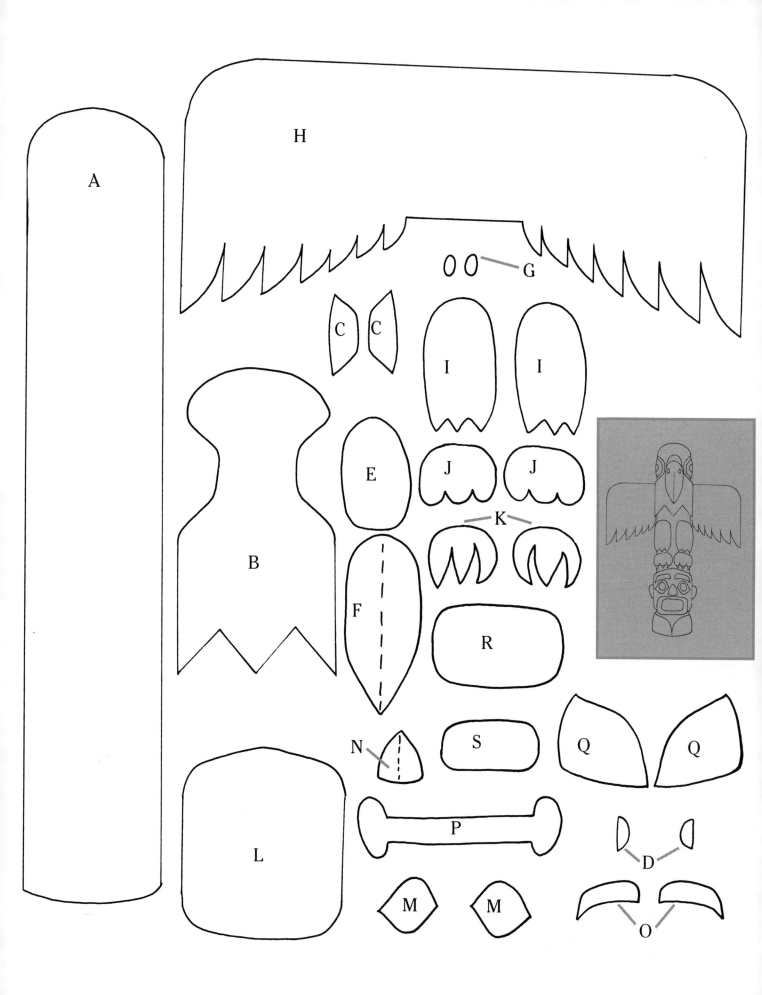

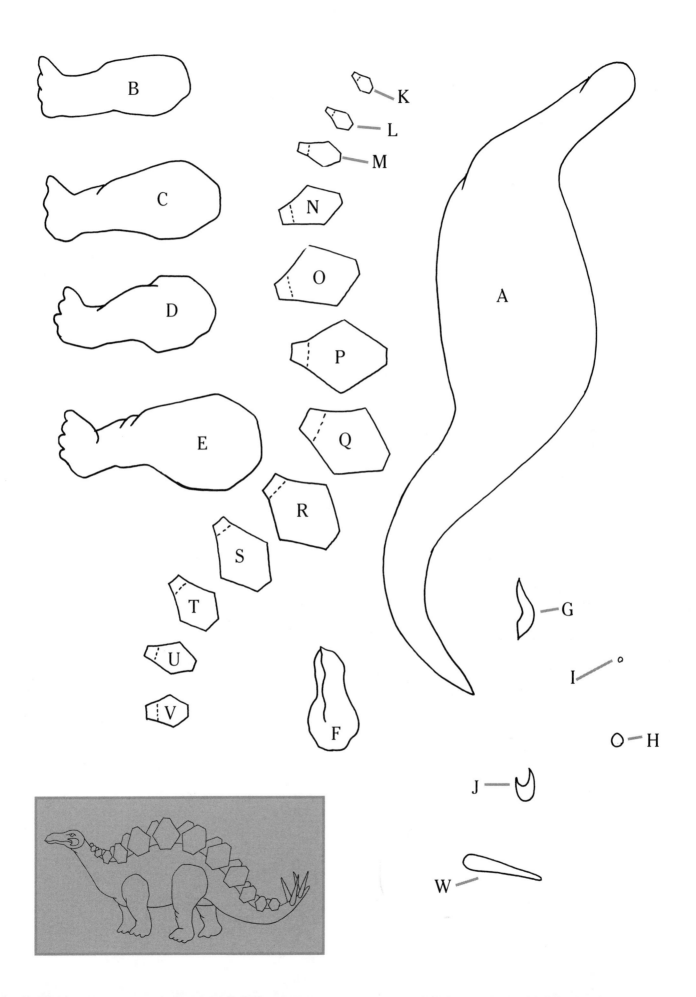

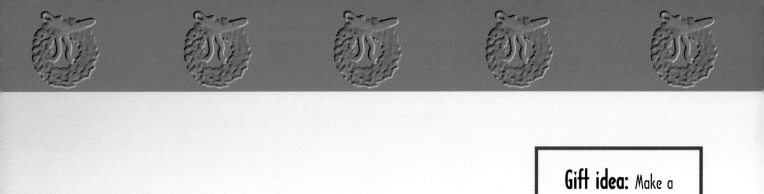

Gift idea: Make a Christmas card your friends will remember. Just glue the wreath to a piece of Bristol board folded in half, and personalize. Or, attach a loop of string to the back to make a Christmas tree decoration.

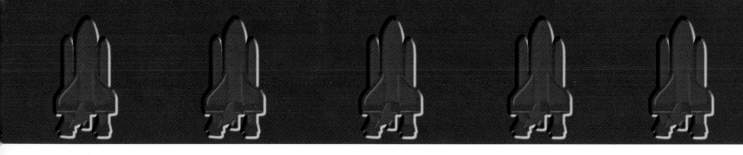

Blast Off!

To give this space shuttle nice straight edges, use a ruler to help you trace and score. Try using a butter-knife blade for crisp score lines.

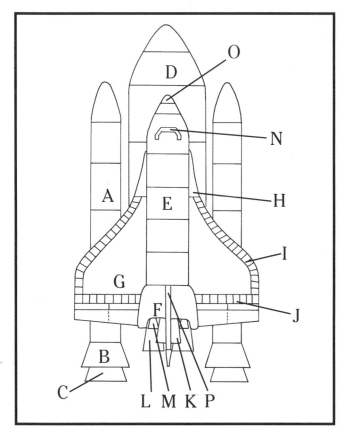

▸ Cut out two copies of **A** (rocket boosters). With clean sides up, score along dotted lines. Then turn them clean side down and curl them till they're rounded (see photo 1).

▸ Cut out two copies each of **B** and **C**. With clean sides down, curl them till they're rounded.

▸ Now assemble the two rocket boosters: for each one, glue **B** behind **A**, and **C** behind **B**. Set them aside.

▸ With clean sides up, score **D** (external tank) and **E** (orbiter) along dotted lines. Then turn them clean side down and curl them till they're rounded.

▸ With clean side down, curl **F**. Glue to **E**, lining up its top edge with the bottom score line.

▸ With clean side up, score **G** (wings) along dotted lines. Burnish around all edges of **H**, then glue **H** to **G**, lining up the two pieces at the top.

▸ With clean sides down, score **I** and **J** pieces (wing trim) along dotted lines. Glue them into place on the wings, and rescore over the raised lines (see photo 2). Then turn wings clean side down and burnish around all edges except the bottom.

▸ With clean sides up, score **K** and two copies of **L** (engines) along dotted lines. Then turn them clean side down and curl them. With clean sides down, curl two copies of **M**.

▸ Now attach the engines to the shuttle. Glue both **M** pieces behind F. Then glue **K** behind **F** as well, between **M** pieces. Finally,

glue both **L** pieces to **G** (wings) so they peek out at the bottom. Spread a very small amount of glue along the edges of the shuttle body, and gently glue to the wings.

▸ With clean side down, curl **N** (window) and **O** (nose cone). Glue to shuttle body.

▸ With clean side down, score **P** (rudder) along dotted lines. To form the rudder, fold along the score lines and glue the two halves together. Spread a very small amount of glue along the shortest edge and glue it to **F**. Hold it in place until dry, about 30 seconds.

▸ Finally, assemble the space shuttle. Glue the two rocket boosters behind the wings,

then glue the finished shuttle to the external tank.

▸ Decorate as you wish. To display your shuttle, glue a popsicle stick to the back, then build a base of crumpled-up aluminum foil around it. This shuttle is decorated with coloured foil flames and cotton ball smoke!

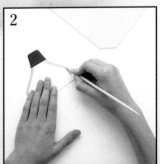

17

Horse Play

Here's a perfect gift for any horse lover.

▸ With clean side down, curl **A** (neck). Burnish around all cut edges. Curl the smaller neck section a little more.

▸ With clean side down, curl **B** (head). Burnish around all edges, adding a little extra burnishing to the bottom lip. With clean side down, curl and burnish around all edges of **C**. Then turn clean side up and glue **B** on top of it. (Only a bit of **C** will show.)

▸ With clean side down, burnish around all edges of **D** except the nostril curl. Burnish heavily around the brow area. Turn clean side up and use the burnisher to *indent* the nostril slightly.

▸ Now make the eyes. With clean side down, burnish around all edges of **E** (eye) and **F** (pupil). Glue pupil to eye, and glue eye behind the brow area of **D**. Then glue **D** to the head, lining up their top edges.

▸ Glue the head to the neck. Hold it in place until dry, about 30 seconds.

▸ Now make the horse's forelock. With clean sides down, curl **G**, **H**, **I** and **J** and burnish around all edges. Turn them clean side up and curl forelock tips up slightly. Glue them into place one by one, from right to left.

▸ Follow the same steps for the mane. Curl and burnish **K**, **L**, **M** and **N**, as above. Glue them into place on the neck one by one, from left to right.

▸ With clean side down, burnish around all cut edges of **O** (ear). Burnish the thinner part of the ear, then turn it clean side up and burnish the wider part (see photo).

Put a small dot of glue on the right flap. Tuck it behind the left flap and hold it in place until dry, about 30 seconds. Glue the ear to the head.

Gift idea: Make a picture frame for your horse! (Ask an adult to help you.) Cut four pieces of thick cardboard into equal-sized rectangles. Cut a rectangle out of the middle of one to make the top layer of the frame. Cut bigger rectangles out of the next two — these narrower frames will go underneath the top layer. Leave the last one uncut — this will be the base of the frame. Glue the two middle layers to the base, then finish with the top layer. Score the corners diagonally, as shown, and glue horse in place. Hang the frame on a wall, or make a simple triangular cardboard display stand (see left).

Fly-Catching Frog

The fly in this sculpture has realistic-looking wings — made from tracing paper!
Hint: mark arm and leg pieces with "left" and "right"
so you'll remember which is which.

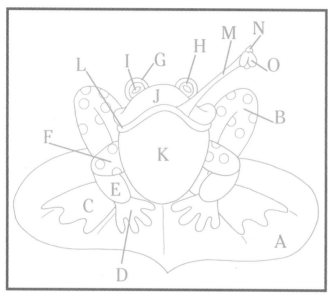

▶ With clean side up, score **A** (lily pad) along dotted lines. Then turn it clean side down and burnish around all edges.

▶ Give the frog spots: glue paper dots to the clean sides of both **B** pieces (legs). Then turn legs clean side down and curl.

▶ Put a small drop of glue on the outside half of each leg and glue behind the inside half. Hold in place until dry, about 30 seconds.

▶ With clean side down, burnish **C** pieces (feet) along dotted lines. Then turn it clean side up and burnish between raised lines.

Glue feet to legs. Glue feet and legs to lily pad.

▶ With clean sides down, burnish around all edges of **D** pieces (hands). Turn them clean side up and curl the "wrists" lightly.

▶ Now put the frog's "arms" together. Glue paper dots to **F** pieces, as you did with legs. With clean sides down, curl all **E** and **F** pieces. Glue forearms to hands, and arms to forearms (see photo 1). Set aside.

▶ Now for the eyes. With clean side down, burnish around all edges of **G**. With clean side down, burnish **H** pieces (eyeballs) with a circular motion, from outside to centre. Glue them to **G**. Glue **I** pieces (pupils) to eyeballs, or simply draw them on.

▶ With clean side down, burnish around all edges of **J** (upper lip). Glue eyes to the back of this piece.

▶ With clean side down, curl **K** (chest) until it's very rounded. Set aside.

▶ With clean side down, curl and burnish around all edges of **L** (bottom lip). Glue bottom lip to chest, then upper lip to bottom lip, one corner at a time. Leave a slight gap between the lips (see photo 2).

20

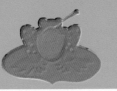

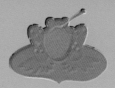

Glue arms to chest. Then glue finished body to legs.

▸ Make two copies of **M** (tongue). Turn them clean side down, and burnish along their dotted lines. Glue one behind the other (make a double thickness). Glue tongue to mouth, tucking its base behind the lower lip.

▸ With clean side down, curl **N** (fly body). Glue **O** (tracing-paper wings) to fly body. Glue fly to tongue.

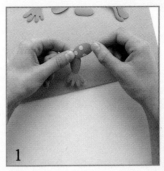

Totem Pole

A striking West Coast symbol inspired this attractive — and useful — desk topper.

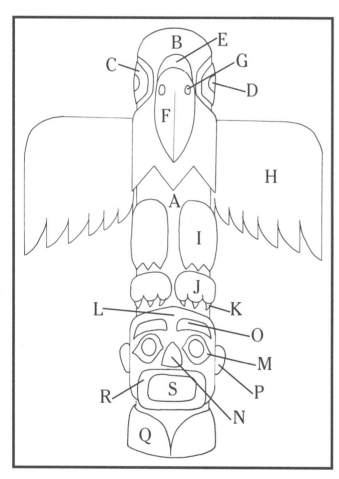

▸ With clean side down, curl **A** (pole). Then, with clean side down, curl **B** (eagle head). Burnish around all edges except the bottom. Glue it to the pole, lining up their top edges.

▸ With clean sides down, burnish around all edges of both **C** pieces (eagle eyes). Glue **D** pieces (eagle pupils) to eyes. Glue finished eyes to the pole.

▸ Now make the eagle's beak. With clean side down, curl and burnish around all edges of **E** (beak base). With clean side down, curl and burnish around all edges of **F** (beak). Score along dotted line and pinch to shape. Glue both **G** pieces (nostrils) to the beak. With clean side down, spread a small amount of glue along the top edge of the beak. Glue to base. Glue the finished beak to the eagle head.

▸ With clean side down, burnish along straight edge of **H** (wings). Then turn the piece clean side up and gently curl each wing, so the feather tips curl up. Glue the wings to the back of the pole.

▸ With clean sides down, curl and burnish around all edges of both **I** pieces (legs). Glue them to the pole beneath the eagle head.

▸ With clean sides down, curl and burnish around all edges of both **J** pieces (feet). Glue both **K** pieces (claws) behind feet. Glue the completed feet to the pole beneath the eagle legs.

▸ With clean side down, curl and burnish around all edges of **L** (head). Glue it to the pole beneath the eagle claws.

▸ With clean sides up, gently burnish the centres of both **M** pieces (eyes), so their edges curl up. Punch out paper dots for

Gift idea: Make a pencil holder! Decorate an empty toilet-paper roll with paper strips. Glue it to the back of the totem pole. Cut out a paper circle for the base and glue it to the bottom of the roll.

pupils. Burnish each one with a circular motion, from outside to centre. Glue them to the eyes. Glue the finished eyes to the head.

▶ With clean side down, curl **N** (nose). Score along dotted line and pinch to shape. Glue it to the head.

▶ With clean sides down, burnish all edges of both **O** pieces (eyebrows). Glue into place.

▶ With clean side up, burnish **P** (ears). Glue the piece into place behind the pole so the ears curl forward.

▶ With clean sides down, curl and burnish around all edges of both **Q** pieces (blanket). Glue them to the pole, overlapping their edges slightly.

▶ With clean side up, curl **R** (mouth). Then turn clean side down and burnish around all edges (see photo).

▶ With clean side up, curl **S** (mouth opening). Glue to centre of mouth. Glue finished mouth to head.

Mega Stegosaurus

If you make its legs with a firm paper (you can even use old greeting cards), this dino will stand on its own.

▶ With clean side down, curl **A** (body) from the neck to the tail (see photo 1). Burnish around all edges.

▶ With clean side down, curl **B**, **C**, **D** and **E** (legs) till they're nice and round. Burnish around all cut edges. Glue **B** and **D** behind the body, and **C** and **E** onto the front of the body.

▶ With clean sides down, curl and burnish around all edges of **F** (head) and **G** (brow).

▶ Make an eye: burnish **H** with a circular motion, from outside to centre. Glue on **I** (pupil) or simply draw one on.

▶ Now build the head. Glue the finished eye behind the brow, then glue the brow to the

head. With clean side down, curl **J** (cheek) and glue it in place on the head. Glue the finished head to the body.

▶ Now add the stegosaurus's bony plates. With clean sides down, score **K** through **V**, fold along the score lines, and glue the flaps to the front of the body, just below the edge of the back (see photo 2). Then cut out another set of plates, **K** through **V**, and score and fold them as before. Glue these ones to the *back* of the body, so they're visible between the front plates.

▶ Finally, add the tail spikes. Cut out four **W** shapes; with clean sides down, curl and pinch them to shape. Glue two to the back of the tail, and two to the front.

1

2

Rattlesnake Warning!

Watch out — this lifelike rattler might bite!

▸ First, glue diamond patterns to the snake's body:
Decorate **A** with **B** and **C**.
Decorate **D** with **E** and **F**.
Decorate **G** with **H** and **I**.
Decorate **J** with **K** and **L**.

▸ With clean sides down, curl **A**, **D**, **G** and **J** until they're nicely rounded. Burnish around all wavy cut edges — these are the snake's belly ridges (see photo 1).

▸ Now start the head. With clean side down, burnish bottom edge of **M**. With clean side down, score **N** along dotted line and pinch gently to shape. Burnish its top edge. With clean side down, burnish bottom edge of **O**.

Glue **O** to **N**, lining them up *at the bottom*. Glue **P** to **O**, lining them up *at the top*.

▸ Put together the eye: with clean side down, burnish **Q** (eye) with a circular motion, from outside to centre. Glue it to the snake's head. Glue **R** (pupil) to the eye, or simply draw one on. With clean side down, burnish around all edges of **S** (eyelid). Glue it over the eye.

▸ Curl **T** (tongue), one centimetre-long section at a time — one section clean side up, the next clean side down, and so on, to give the tongue a realistic wavy shape. Glue the tongue behind **O**. Then finish the head by gluing **M** behind it, so only a narrow strip is visible along the jaw.

▸ With clean side up, score **U** (rattle) along dotted lines (see photo 2). Then turn it clean side down and burnish each section between score lines. Glue to **J**.

▸ Now you're ready to glue the body sections together. (Before you start gluing, have a good look at the project outline and photo to see how everything fits together.)
Glue the head to **D** (neck coil).
Glue **D** over **A** (rear coil).
Glue **G** (middle coil) over **D**.
Glue **J** (tail coil) over **G**.

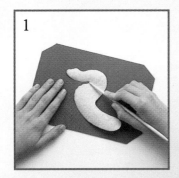

Gift idea: Make a cool "Keep Out" poster by gluing your finished rattlesnake to a cardboard backing. Decorate as you wish.

This finished spread shows you just how far you can go!

    To achieve these results, I used watercolour paper and paint, but the sculpting techniques I used are much the same as the ones you have learned in this book.

    This sculpture may look very complicated, but it's really just many simple

pieces built up together. Look carefully at each part of the sculpture and try to figure out how I might have made it. Then try to imagine how I might have put the parts together. You're probably on the right track!

Happy sculpting . . .

To my wife, Joanne Webb, for without her push and patience,
this book may never have happened. Thank you for all your help.
R.B.

For my nephews: Matthew, Daniel, Aaron and Christopher.
J.W.

Special thanks to Sarnia's Lakeroad School
Grade 6 Class of `96 for helping us develop these projects.

The publishers wish to thank Suzanne and Lindsey Nigra for helping to test the projects,
and Jordan Caughers for appearing in the photographs.

Joanne Webb started writing when she received her first laptop computer. She enjoys reading, music and animals. When she's not creating children's story ideas and being a full-time mom, Joanne visits hospitals and nursing homes with her dog as a St. John Ambulance Pet Therapy volunteer.

Ron Broda's amazing paper sculptures have been intriguing kids for years. His first book, *The Little Crooked Christmas Tree*, was published in 1990, and has since become a holiday classic. Ron is currently the curator of Discovery House, a children's museum in Sarnia, Ontario.

Ron and Joanne live in Sarnia with their children and a Great Dane named Shane.

Other books illustrated by Ron Broda:

· *The Little Crooked Christmas Tree*, written by Michael Cutting
Waters, written by Edith Newlin Chase
Have You Seen Bugs?, written by Joanne Oppenheim